MR.BRAVE

by Roger Hargreaves

PSS!
PRICE STERN SLOAN

Mr. Brave is not as strong as Mr. Strong.

He is not as tall as Mr. Tall.

But that does not stop him being brave, as you will soon see.

Now, last Tuesday, Little Miss Bossy invited Mr. Brave to tea.

"AND DON'T BE LATE!" she shouted over the phone.

It was a very stormy day, but Mr. Brave knew that Little Miss Bossy's temper was worse than the storm.

So he set off for Little Miss Bossy's house, hurrying along as fast as he could, to be sure that he was not late for tea.

Along the way he heard a cry for help.

It was Mr. Messy.

He had been blown into the river by the wind.

Mr. Brave did not want to be late to see Little Miss Bossy, but being the brave fellow he was, he jumped into the river and rescued Mr. Messy.

Sopping wet, Mr. Brave hurried along the road.

Suddenly, he heard someone loudly sobbing.

Who could it be?

It was Little Miss Somersault!

She was balancing on a tightrope tied between two tall trees!

"Oh, Mr. Brave, I'm so lonely," she sobbed. "Nobody will come and play on my tightrope! They are all too frightened of heights. You're so brave, won't you come and join me?"

Mr. Brave looked up at Little Miss Somersault.

Then he thought about Little Miss Bossy, but being the brave fellow he was, he took pity on Little Miss Somersault and climbed onto the tightrope.

They chitchatted happily until Mr. Brave happened to look down.

"Little Miss Somersault! Look! The rope is going to snap! We're going to fall . . . and it's such a long way to the bottom. Oh, calamity! Oh, help!" he cried out in panic.

"Be brave, Mr. Brave," said Little Miss Somersault.

With no more fuss, she carried him safely back down to the ground.

"Oh, thank you," said Mr. Brave with a sigh of relief.

Little Miss Somersault said good-bye.

And Mr. Brave was left on his own, shaking like a leaf.

"I don't deserve to be called Mr. Brave. I was scared stiff! Thank goodness nobody knows my secret," he said to himself.

And nobody did know his secret, or did they?

Little Miss Trouble just happened to be passing by. She saw everything.

And what she had seen and heard had given her an idea.

A very naughty idea!

She grinned a mischievous grin.

"Hey! Come here everybody! Come and see this!" she shouted at the top of her voice.

Very quickly, a large crowd gathered.

"I have an announcement," announced Little Miss Trouble. "Did you know that Mr. Brave isn't brave at all?"

"No, it can't be true," said the crowd all at once.

"It is true!" said Little Miss Trouble, "and I'll prove it to you."

"Mr. Brave," she continued, "I dare you to walk across that tightrope!"

Mr. Brave looked up at the tightrope.

And all the crowd looked up at the tightrope.

Then all the crowd looked at Mr. Brave.

Mr. Brave suddenly remembered something.

A very important something.

"Just look at the time!" he cried. "I'm going to be late for tea at Little Miss Bossy's!"

"Gotta run!" he cried.

And he ran off as quickly as possible.

"Hooray!" cheered the crowd.

And they all clapped and applauded Mr. Brave.

Little Miss Trouble looked very puzzled.

"Why are you all cheering him?" she cried. "He ran away! He isn't brave at all!"

"Oh, yes he is!" they all shouted. "Would you show up late for tea at Little Miss Bossy's house?"

Little Miss Trouble thought for a moment.
"Gosh, he is brave after all!" she said in awe.